ADVENTURE DUCK

VS

THE WICKED WALRUS

ORCHARD BOOKS

First published in Great Britain in 2020 by The Watts Publishing Group

3 5 7 9 10 8 6 4

Text copyright © Orchard Books 2020
Illustrations copyright © Orchard Books 2020

Designed by Arvind Shah

A CIP catalogue record for this book is available from the British Library.

ISBN 978 1 40835 687 6

Printed and bound in Great Britain by
Clays Ltd Elcograf S.p.A.

The paper and board used in this book are made from
wood from responsible sources.

Orchard Books
An imprint of Hachette Children's Group
Part of The Watts Publishing Group Limited
Carmelite House, 50 Victoria Embankment, London EC4Y 0DZ

An Hachette UK Company
www.hachette.co.uk
www.hachettechildrens.co.uk

ADVENTURE DUCK

VS THE WICKED WALRUS

BY STEVE COLE

ILLUSTRATED BY ALEKSEI BITSKOFF

ORCHARD

OFF to the Arctic!

Down in the park, a duck and a zebra were hiding in a tree.

"It's hard work being a superhero," the duck quacked quietly to his zebra friend. "You have to be on duty ALL the time in case danger's afoot."

"Danger is afoot," the zebra agreed. "*MY FOOT!*" She clomped him on the head with a hoof. "*Geddit?*"

The duck – who was called

Adventure Duck (or A.D.

for short) – frowned at his companion. "No,
Ziggy, I mean, danger is afoot over there."
He pointed across the park. A small boy
was eating an ice lolly but it was melting
fast and about to slip off its stick.

WHOOSH*!* Adventure Duck burst

from the tree at supersonic speed, caught
the falling ice lolly neatly with one

webbed foot and flicked it back into the boy's mouth.

Then – **ZOOM!** – A.D. whizzed back to the tree, smirking proudly. "Impressive, huh, Zig? Er, Zig … ?"

The zebra had vanished from the tree.

"Over here!" she brayed.

A.D. saw Ziggy in the car park, standing beside a car with its bonnet up.

"This thing has a flat battery and is in great danger of going nowhere," she explained. "But that battery won't be flat for long, thanks to the amazing electro-powers of ... **NEON ZEBRA-RAH-RAH-RAH!**" Ziggy's stripes glowed pink and she put both of her front hooves against the battery. *ZAPPP!* Sparks shot out, and the car's engine suddenly roared into life.

"Not bad," A.D. admitted, joining his friend as she walked back towards the duck pond. "It's nice to use our powers to help out around the park. But what I really want is some proper action ..."

"*YOU WISH FOR ACTION?*" A large, levitating egg burst out from beneath the pond-water. "Your wish may come true!"

The egg's name was YOKI – and he was their boss. He was speckled green, with wise eyes and a bushy moustache that could win prizes. With his mystical powers, the clever egg could sense trouble anywhere in the world – and send A.D. and Ziggy to sort it out.

"You've been working on your dramatic entrances, Yoki!" Ziggy beamed approvingly. "Cool."

"Now, if it is coolness you crave, join me in the Underpond,'" said Yoki. "I have something **extremely cold** to show you ..." Waggling his moustache, the jumbo egg sank back down beneath the surface of the water.

"I hate it when he acts mysterious," Adventure Duck grumbled.

- - - - -

They ran to the edge of the pond and Ziggy pulled on a lever hidden in the reeds. The ground flipped upside down and dropped them into a muddy, underground chamber – Yoki's secret base, *THE UNDERPOND*.

It was filled with all kinds of high-tech gadgets, from consoles and computer screens to an enormous TV. In the middle of the feathery floor stood a large black globe. Yoki was floating in front of it, watching as a red light flashed on and off near the North Pole.

"What's going on?" asked A.D. "Don't tell me Rudolph crashed a sleigh and he's signalling for help!"

- - - - -

"No." Yoki sighed heavily. "The light means that my sensors have detected **meteor mutants** in the Arctic Circle."

"Meteor mutants like us," breathed Ziggy.

Yoki, Neon Zebra and Adventure Duck had gained their superpowers from mysterious chunks of space rock. They used their abilities for good – but not all the animals affected by the meteor did the same …

"Any meteor mutants in the Arctic Circle must be frozen solid, right?" said A.D., perched on a comfy chair. "No problem to anyone."

- - - - -

"I'm afraid not." Yoki nodded to a map on the computer screen. It showed an icy wasteland, with vast blue cliffs looming high over a grey sea. "Strange things are happening in the Arctic. My super-sensitive moustache has detected vibrations in the ice." The ends of Yoki's moustache pointed due north and quivered in alarm.

"What's causing the vibrations?" asked Ziggy.

"A polar bear rock concert?" A.D. suggested.

Yoki gave him a hardboiled stare. "No. They are not good vibrations."

Ziggy shrugged. "Then, what?"

"Even my incredible knowledge has its limits," Yoki admitted. "However, I sense terrible danger and perilous ... um, peril. The two of you must journey to the North Pole and learn more!"

"**WHAT**? But it's **FREEZING** at the North Pole!" A.D. turned to Ziggy. "What sane, self-respecting duck would ever agree to go there?"

Yoki raised an eyebrow. "You are not sane, and you know nothing about respect."

"You're right!" cried A.D. "OK, I guess I

- - - - -

am going to the North Pole."

"But I'm from Africa!" Ziggy declared. "I need the sun! **WARMTH!**"

"Neither of you will feel the cold." Yoki crossed to the cupboard and pulled out a red cape and a bandana with a lightning bolt on it. "I have created special insulated versions of your super-costumes that will keep you toasty warm."

"**NICE FOR THE ICE!**" A.D. grabbed the cape and swished it about. "You're wasted as Earth's guardian, egg. You should be a fashion designer! Mmm, I can't wait to rock these cosy threads."

- - - - -

Ziggy happily put on her bandana. "This really brings out the colour of my eyes."

"Then it is settled." Yoki smiled, his moustache twitching with pride. "You will embark on this vital Arctic expedition – **at once!**"

Where No Duck or Zebra Have Gone Before

The journey to the North Pole was long, through icy winds and snowstorms. Adventure Duck tied a long, woolly scarf around Neon Zebra's middle and towed her through the air. She fired up her stripes to a bright red to light their way. Just as Yoki had promised, the high-tech fabric somehow protected their whole bodies from the worst of the cold.

- - - - - -

Adventure Duck wished he had earmuffs. Not just because his ears were cold, but to shut out Ziggy's terrible singing! She loved making up songs to pass long journeys, but A.D. was **NOT** a fan of her work.

"Ziggy the red-striped zebraaaaaaaaaaaaa,

Had a very stripy butt!

And if you ever saw it,

She would hit you on the nut!"

"PUT A SOCK IN IT!" yelled Adventure Duck.

"Put a sock in my **BUTT?**" asked Ziggy. **"EWW!"**

"No, I mean, shush!" A.D. groaned. "I think we're nearly there."

"You are indeed, young duck!" Yoki's voice boomed through A.D.'s head. They shared a kind of *Eggs-tra Sensory Perception* that meant they could talk to each other with their minds, even over long distances. "Your landing site is just ahead. Begin your descent!"

Adventure Duck immediately dropped Ziggy and she fell like a stripy rock, landing in a snowdrift. "Nice descent, Zig!"

"That is not what I meant," said Yoki wearily.

With a chuckle, A.D. fluffed up his tail feathers ready for landing. As he did so, he noticed a large white bird fly up for a closer look at him. It had a strange green stripe between its beady eyes.

"Hi. I'm Adventure Duck," said A.D. "Basically the coolest, and yet surprisingly toasty, super-bird you'll ever see. Who are you?"

But the bird ignored him, soaring away again.

"That was an **ARCTIC TERN**," Yoki noted as A.D. got ready to land. "They don't usually have a green stripe like that one."

"Maybe he's into make-up?" said A.D.

Then suddenly – *THUMP!* *BOING!*

- - - - -

– Adventure Duck struck something.
"**YEOWWWWWWW!**" He skittered
over the slippy ice and looked around,
confused. "Yoki? What did I hit? There's
nothing here."

There was no reply – the mystery crash
had broken their ESP link. But even so, the
question was quickly answered.

"I'll tell you what you hit. You hit **ME!**"
Adventure Duck heard heavy hooves on
the ice and suddenly a reindeer with
huge antlers appeared right in front of
him, looking cross. "I was fast asleep!
Do you think it's fun to attack someone
in their sleep?"

- - - - -

"Whoa there! I didn't attack anyone," A.D. protested. "I didn't even see you!"

But the reindeer wasn't listening. **WHAP!** She used her antlers to knock him flying headfirst into a bank of snow. "***OOF!***" he quacked.

"STOP RIGHT THERE, ANTLER-FACE!"

- - - - -

Neon Zebra had freed herself from the snowdrift and galloped over the ice, her stripes sizzling with orange energy.

"**EEK!**" The reindeer's eyes bulged with fright. "**BYE!**"

Suddenly, she vanished.

"*HUH?*" Neon Zebra skidded to a confused stop. "How'd she do that?"

A split second later – **CRACK!** – something crashed into Ziggy's head.

"Look! I see stars," said Ziggy, rubbing her head. "It must be the northern lights."

- - - - -

"Zig!" cried Adventure Duck. "What happened?"

"I guess I did!" The reindeer reappeared and shrugged. "Sorry, not sorry!"

"That does it, moose mush." Crossly, Adventure Duck charged up to the reindeer and gave an ultra-noisy QUACK!

"**Whoa!**" The reindeer did a somersault and landed upside-down on her antlers, which jammed into the ice. "Well, this is kind of embarrassing ..."

BOING

Suddenly, she vanished again.

Ziggy staggered dizzily to her feet.
"Where's she gone *now*?"

A.D. reached out a wing and, though
he couldn't see anything, he felt a furry
head. "She's still here ... but she's just
INVISIBLE!"

"Gerroff," said the reindeer's voice, as her
invisible head shook A.D.'s wing clear. "My
name's **CARRIE** ..." She reappeared and
yelled, "**CARRIE BOO!**"

Adventure Duck and Ziggy jumped.

"Cut that out," said Ziggy crossly. "I'm guessing that you got your power to turn invisible from a lump of space rock. Right?"

"Yes! Wow, good guess," said Carrie Boo. "Wait – did that happen to you too?" When Ziggy and A.D. nodded, Carrie was so surprised she vanished again. From out of nowhere, her voice continued, "I was grazing in Lapland when this meteorite crashed down and gave me the power to turn invisible."

"That's a pretty cool superpower," said Adventure Duck.

- - - - - -

"But I can't control it, especially when I'm afraid," said Carrie. "And it freaked my herd out so they sent me away."

"My herd kicked me out too," said Ziggy, nodding sympathetically. "Just because I kept accidentally frying them with my **electric zaps!**"

"You know what it's like to be an outsider, then?" Carrie reappeared, and there were tears in her eyes. "But you learned to control your powers, right?"

"Yep. And so will you. Although, accidents do happen." Ziggy raised a hoof and zapped Adventure Duck's tail with a

- - - - -

neon-red blast. "**OOPS**. See?"

A.D. plunged his smoking bottom into the snow to cool it, then waddled up to Carrie Boo. "Thing is, deer, the meteorites gave us powers and we use them for good. That makes us **awesome** superheroes. But some animals use their powers for **EVIL**. That makes them supervillains and we have to kick their butts. So – what are you going to do, Carrie?"

"Er ..." Carrie stared past him and gulped. "I'm going to run away."

A.D. frowned. "That doesn't sound very brave. Superheroes *never* run away from danger."

"This time you might want to make an exception," said Carrie. She pointed her hoof at the sky.

A.D. and Ziggy turned to see what she was looking at – and gasped.

An enormous rocket was shooting through the sky – *and heading straight for them*!

A Walrus in a Hovercraft

"Stand aside, guys!" Neon Zebra's stripes pulsed shocking pink and she raised her front hooves as the rocket whooshed closer. "I'll blast it away."

"Nooo!" Adventure Duck whacked her with his wing. "It might blow up and turn us into roast dinners!"

Carrie Boo had turned invisible again, but the others could hear her four knees

- - - - - -

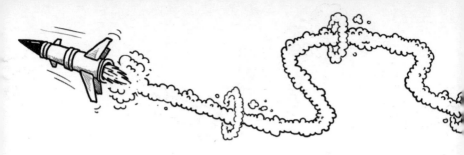

knocking. "**IT'S GOING TO HIT US!**"

But the rocket changed course and started whizzing about the sky like a mad mosquito.

"I'm no expert," said Ziggy, "but I think that thing's out of control!"

The worried animals watched as the rocket went on spiralling. Finally, it smashed down into the snow about a mile away.

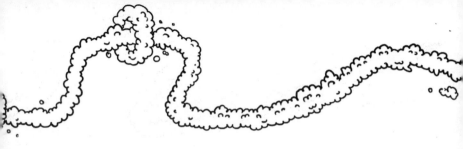

The ground shook and a fireball rose up
into the sky.

"Phew! That was a close call," quacked A.D.

"We were lucky," said Carrie Boo softly.
"But I think that thing came down close
to a human village."

Ziggy frowned. "A village? At the North
Pole?"

Carrie nodded. "There are some humans
living in igloos."

"What's an IGLOO?" A.D. pondered. "A frozen toilet?"

"An igloo is a house made of snow," said Yoki's voice in his mind. "You *must* investigate this village."

"So bossy," A.D. grumbled.

"The vibrations I sensed in the ice could be caused by rockets launching – like that one," said Yoki. "But ... where are they coming from?"

Adventure Duck sighed. "I suppose we have to find out."

- - - - -

"Er, does he always talk to himself?" Carrie whispered to Ziggy.

"He's not talking to himself," explained Ziggy. "He's talking to Yoki."

Carrie frowned. "Who's Yoki?"

"Just this genius floating egg with a moustache we know," Ziggy went on. "He sends us on our missions."

"And Yoki says we need to check out this village," A.D. told the others.

"Lead the way, Carrie," said Ziggy.

- - - - -

A.D. and Ziggy followed the reindeer
through the snow. Trying to ignore his frozen
feet, A.D. looked out over the Arctic, in all its
glittering beauty. He saw something small
hop out from behind a nearby icy boulder. It
was an Arctic hare, white and fluffy – with a
green stripe above its nose, just
like the bird he'd seen earlier.

That's funny, thought
Adventure Duck.
*Green must be the
fashion here.* He was
about to tell Ziggy that
she needed to turn her stripes green if she
wanted to be in style, but the hare jumped
off and was soon lost from sight.

Soon the super-animals reached the village. A cluster of igloos overlooked the half-frozen sea with the enormous blue glacier towering in the distance. People in uniforms were walking around eating ice lollies with enormous smiles on their faces. They looked surprisingly calm, considering their village had nearly been wiped out seconds before.

"Where are they getting those **LOLLIES** from? Since there's no soggy bread around here, I'll give them a try." Adventure Duck waddled over to a lolly lying on the ground. He shoved it in his mouth ... then started flapping around, quacking in pain.

- - - - - -

"What's wrong?"
Carrie
cried.
"Does it
taste bad?"

"No," A.D. squeaked.
"IT JUST GAVE ME BRAIN FREEZE!"

"WAIT. You realise what sort of
lolly that is, don't you?" Ziggy held up
the wrapper, which showed an image
of a pug dressed as an Arctic explorer.
"It's a ***POOCHO ROCKET LOLLY***.
That means it must have been made by
POWER PUG!"

- - - - -

"Ugh," groaned A.D. The pug looked so cute, but was actually deadly dangerous. "I **HATE** that dumb-brained dog!"

Carrie looked at them blankly. "Who is Power Pug?"

"He used to be just the mascot for Poocho, Inc," Ziggy explained. "It's a massive company that sells food and drink all around the world."

"One of the special meteorites made him *super-brainy*," A.D. went on. "So he hypnotised his owner and took control of the company. He's using it to try and take over the whole world."

- - - - - -

"And you think this little dog is behind the strange events here?" asked Carrie Boo.

"Could be," said Ziggy. "What are these people doing out here – besides eating ice lollies, I mean?"

Carrie walked up to a man in a peaked cap, who had a card on a strap around his neck. **"TOP SECRET SPACE BASE,"** she read aloud.

A.D. looked around. All of the humans had those ID cards around their necks. "This doesn't *look* like a Top Secret Space Base to me. Everyone's just wandering round eating lollies." He took another lick of his ice lolly

and shook his head, feeling strangely dizzy.
"I'd better tell Yoki about all this ..."

A.D. closed his eyes and tried to concentrate,
but his dizziness was getting worse. "Egg – are
you there? What can you tell us about a Top
Secret Space Base at the North Pole?"
There was no reply. "Dumb egg ..."

"**SHHH***!*" Ziggy hissed. "I hear something ..."

A.D. listened, and sure enough heard a hum of
power. A high-tech hovercraft was gliding over
the sea! "Ooooh, cool!"

As the craft drew nearer, they saw two things.
Firstly, that TOP SECRET SPACE BASE

- - - - - -

was written on its side. Secondly, the
driver was an **ENORMOUS, BLUBBERY
ANIMAL** with two fat flippers.

He wore a sailor hat. Giant tusks hung
down from the creature's mouth, which
was half hidden by a gigantic moustache.
"What *IS* that?" asked Adventure Duck.

"It's a *walrus*!" said Carrie. "But I don't think

it's an *ordinary* walrus."

"Oh, *really*?" said Ziggy. "What gave it away
– the fact that he's driving a hovercraft?"
The zebra shooed her friends behind the
nearest igloo. "Come on, hide!"

A.D. giggled and stood still. His eyes had
glazed over and he was smiling strangely.

"Shift your feathery butt!" Ziggy hissed,
giving him a shove.

The strange craft left the water and
glided up over the icy shore. The walrus
flopped out and dragged itself towards
the humans.

- - - - -

"Why aren't they freaking out at the sight of him?" Ziggy whispered.

"Hear me, humans!" the walrus bellowed, his fat-rolls quivering. "I did not expect that test rocket to land so close to you," he boomed. "To apologise, I have brought you *more* Poocho rocket lollies – **THE ICY TREAT THAT'S HARD TO BEAT**." He reached into his hovercraft and started tossing the ice lollies at the humans like it was feeding time at the zoo.

"So *he's* the one giving them lollies," breathed Ziggy.

"What if he sees us?" Carrie quivered.

- - - - - -

"Just chill, m'deer!" Adventure Duck had a silly smile on his beak as the humans helped themselves to the lollies. "You really should try one. They *do* make you feel calmer. *Good old Poocho rocket lollies.* **Good old Power Pug**!"

"**WHAT?**" Ziggy hissed. "What is *wrong* with you, duck?"

"I'm just **TOO COOOOOL!**" A. D. shouted.

"**SHHHH!**" hissed Carrie, suddenly turning invisible.

"**WHO'S THERE**?" the huge walrus

- - - - -

snarled. Lumbering forwards, he smashed through the igloo – revealing Ziggy and A.D.

Slowly, threateningly, the walrus wobbled towards them ...

Tidal Wave of Terror

"**Well, well**," hissed the whopping walrus. "If it isn't Adventure Duck and Neon Zebra."

"I'm confused." A.D. frowned dizzily. "If it *isn't* us, *who* is it?"

"It IS us," Ziggy said boldly. "Remember our rhyme? NEON ZEBRA AND ADVENTURE DUCK – HERE TO SAY, YOU'RE OUT OF LUCK!"

- - - - -

"SILENCE!" the walrus growled. "Nothing must interfere with my plans – **HIIII-YAAH!"** He flapped out his flippers in a double karate strike!

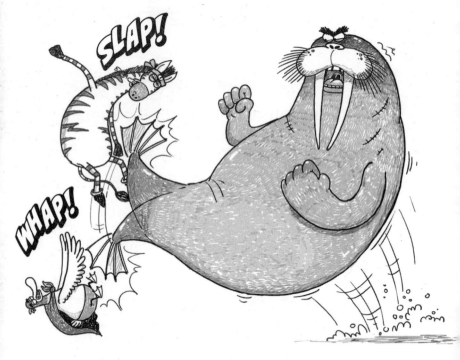

Ziggy and A.D. were sent flying into the snow. Before either of them could move, the wicked walrus waddled towards them.

Ziggy stared in horror. "He's going to spear us with his tusks and squash us flat with his fat."

"Can we choose which one he does first?" A.D. asked cheerily.

But then a noise like thunder rolled across from the horizon – KRAKKOOOOOOOM!

The walrus looked up sharply. "*Oh, no – the glacier!* My latest rocket test launch was too much for it ..."

"Huh?" A.D. shook his fuzzy head and

- - - - -

turned to see that mighty chunks of ice were falling off the glacier and crashing into the sea. "**whoa!** That doesn't look good."

"**CURSES!** I must return to the base and check my calculations!" Leaving Ziggy and A.D. where they lay, the walrus skidded back to his hovercraft. "Humans, return to your igloos at once!" he ordered. "And Duck, Zebra, be warned – **IF WE MEET AGAIN I SHALL SHOW YOU NO MERCY!**" The walrus fired up the hovercraft with a flipper and scooted away over the sea.

"Well, that was weird." Ziggy scrambled

- - - - -

back up to her hooves. "Why did he take off in such a hurry?"

Carrie became visible again. "I'm sorry. I was no help at all." She hung her head so low that snow got up her nose. "I was **SOOOOO** scared. I've never met a walrus like that before."

"Don't worry about it." Adventure Duck put a comforting wing around the reindeer. "*And definitely don't worry about that* **gigantic tidal wave** *that's heading straight for us!*"

"**Whaaaaaaaat?**" Ziggy's stripes burned bright yellow with shock.

- - - - -

A frothing wall of water had risen from the ocean and it was heading towards them.

"The ice that fell from the glacier started a tidal wave!" cried Carrie. "It could wash this entire village away."

"WE HAVE TO DO SOMETHING!"

shouted Ziggy. The wave was thirty metres high now. If it crashed on the shore, it would drown them all.

"Doesn't it look lovely?" A.D. stood on his head.

"It looks even better upside down!"

"Come on, Carrie, *think*," said Ziggy. "How do we snap Adventure Duck out of this trance?"

"Try giving him a shock." Carrie shunted her antlers under A.D.'s behind and flicked her head, hurling him high up in the air. ***"Zap him, Ziggy! NOW!"***

Neon Zebra's stripes glowed bright pink and she let loose a mega-bright blast from her front hooves. Adventure Duck lit up like an X-ray. His eyes bulged as he gave an *EAR-SPLITTING, THUNDERING, MEGA-SUPER-ULTRA-HYPER-*

- - - - -

QUAAAAAA

The quack was so loud it shook the heavens. It was hard enough and loud enough to break the tidal wave apart! Heavy drops of seawater splattered down like rain. Ziggy and Carrie Boo were washed up against a nearby igloo but Carrie managed to catch A.D. as he fell back down to earth.

Neon Zebra strained harder than ever before, until her stripes glowed neon purple. Then, flat on her back, she stuck all four hooves into the air and unleashed not just energy but *HEAT*. The falling ocean water sizzled and steamed as it evaporated

- - - - -

in the neon haze. Then she closed her eyes, exhausted, and her stripes turned dull blue.

"**YOU DID IT!**" Carrie beamed, looking around. "**YOU SAVED THE VILLAGE!**" Sure enough, the igloos had survived. Humans licking ice lollies strolled out of them, looking totally unconcerned.

"**Whoa!**" A.D. wriggled out of Carrie's grip. "What happened? The last thing I remember is an ice lolly giving me brain freeze."

"It gave you more than that," said Carrie. "You went weird and super-chilled, like all the humans here."

"I couldn't even get in touch with Yoki."
Adventure Duck tried to call out to the egg
using his ESP connection, but again there
was no reply.

"You know what I think?" said Ziggy.
"I THINK THESE LOLLIES MESS WITH YOUR MIND."

Carrie nodded. "That would explain why
these space base workers are taking
orders from a walrus."

"Only a big shock can snap you out of it,"
said Ziggy slowly. "That's why the walrus
gave out more ice lollies after the rocket
crashed – in case it had shaken these
guys awake!"

- - - - -

"Hmm ... Makes me wonder what's going on over at that space base," said A.D.

"Well," said Ziggy. "You know what we have to do."

"Go home immediately," A.D. suggested.

"**NO!**" Ziggy biffed his wing. "We have to follow that walrus and investigate the space base."

"Oh, all right, then." Adventure Duck jumped to his webbed feet. "Come on, you two – **let's go!**"

Lair of the Wicked Walrus

"How are we going to find this space base?" asked Carrie.

"Simple! We'll ask for directions." A.D. bustled up to woman in a space base uniform. "Can you direct me to the Top Secret Space Base, please?"

"Sure!" The woman smiled blissfully.

"Head north and you'll find it around the back of the big glacier." She pointed with her lolly, then grinned and waved. "Have a nice day!"

"So much for *top secret,*" said Ziggy. "But hold on, Duckie – how are we going to cross that sea? You can't carry both of us at once, can you?"

"Not that far," Adventure Duck admitted. "But then I don't think I'll have to." He grinned. "It's time you two learned how to **WATER-SKI!**"

Ziggy and Carrie stood on surfboard-sized pieces of ice at the water's edge. Adventure Duck wrapped his long scarf around them like a harness, then took off into the air, towing both Ziggy and Carrie behind him.

"**WOO-HOOOO!**" cried Ziggy, splashing through the freezing surf.

Carrie did a funky butt-wiggle as she rode her ice-board. "**CAN CARRIE BOO DO IT? YES, SHE CAN!**"

It took just a few minutes to arrive at the glacier. Adventure Duck towed his friends to a nearby ice floe and they all came ashore.

"*Aha*," said, Ziggy pointing with her hoof. "I spy tracks in the snow."

A.D. nodded. "Looks like they were left by that walrus's hovercraft."

"There's something else, too." Carrie peered down at a set of bird tracks, puzzled. Weirdly, the tiny bird tracks turned into huge paw-prints that led away across the snow. "What do you supposed happened here?"

"Looks like a bird came too close to a polar bear and got gobbled up," Ziggy said.

"What are you two, *nature detectives*?" A.D. complained. "We've got a space base to find!" He took off again into the grey sky to scout out the area. Looking down, he saw a series of steel domes huddled together in the distance, beside what looked like an enormous launch pad. "Hey!" he quacked back to his friends. "I can see the Top Secret Space Base!"

"Are you sure?" Ziggy called.

"Yes – there's a big sign with '**TOP SECRET SPACE BASE**' on it!"

- - - - - -

A.D. said. "There's another building across the way, too."

"What is it?" asked Carrie.

Adventure Duck frowned. The building looked like a factory, but it was impossible to be sure. "I can't see any signs," he reported, landing back beside them. "Maybe it's even more top secret?"

"Or maybe it's the outside toilet," said Ziggy. "Let's find the walrus."

Adventure Duck, Ziggy and Carrie Boo followed the hovercraft's trail. They found it parked outside a metal tunnel that led straight into the Space Base.

"All right, everyone," said A.D., stepping on to the tunnel's metal floor, "keep an eye out for any *traps*."

As soon as he entered the tunnel, an **enormous cage** dropped down from the roof over him.

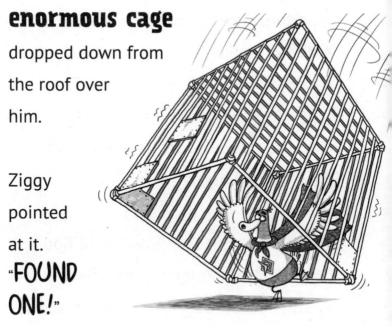

Ziggy pointed at it. "FOUND ONE!"

"This thing is stuck to the floor or something." A.D. strained against the bars, but even his super-strength couldn't budge them. "I can't get free!"

Ziggy was about to lend a hoof when another cage slammed down over her, forcing her down to her stripy knees. **"OW!"**

"OH, NO!" Carrie Boo turned invisible with a squeak of fright. **"WHAT AM I GOING TO DO?"**

"Don't worry, this trap won't hold Neon Zebra for long." Ziggy zapped the cage's bars, but the electricity hit the metal and rebounded back on her. "**YOW!**"

A.D. was growing worried. "Carrie, see if you can find some something to help us break through these bars."

"OK," she whispered. "CARRIE BOO WILL SEE IT THROUGH!"

A.D. heard Carrie's hooves trotting away as a door slid open at the other end of the tunnel and a menacing shadow was revealed.

"Wonderful," groaned Ziggy. "It's you!"

"I'm not a ewe," said the walrus. "**Russ Wall is my name**."

- - - - -

"Russ Wall the Walrus?" A.D. smirked. "I see what you did there."

"**Aha!** You *SEE*, do you?" Russ hissed. "So! You *admit* you are spying!"

"No," said A.D. "I admit you have a dumb name."

"**Do not provoke me!**" Russ held up a remote control in his flipper. He pressed a button and the cages began to slide towards him. "Do you like my magnetic traps? They will take you inside my space base."

"*Your* base?" Ziggy cried. "Don't think so, Russ. You stole it from the poor people who work here."

"Humans do not deserve your pity. People are destroying the ice through global warming." Russ watched as the cages herded the prisoners down the tunnel. "Thanks to human beings, **the whole Earth is heading for disaster!**"

"So you fed the humans here mind-messing lollies, kicked them out of the space base and moved into it yourself?" said Adventure Duck. "How's that going to solve anything?"

The walrus ignored him, wobbling

- - - - -

alongside the cages as they slid into the space base. "The humans were working on a **TOP-SECRET SPACESHIP** that could take a whole army to Mars in just a few days!"

"Wow, that does sound pretty top-secret," A.D. admitted.

"The fools were *years* away from perfecting the rocket boosters," Russ went on. "However, since the meteorite that fell here mutated my mind to *mega-genius levels* ... I've taken over. I have studied the data from each failed launch and fixed every problem. Thanks to my super-clever brain, the rockets are ready now."

- - - - -

"You've caused problems too," Ziggy pointed out. "Bits broke off the glacier after your last test rocket launch."

"No more tests are needed," the walrus informed them. "The glacier is strong enough to withstand one final take-off. Soon, in a blaze of glory, the spaceship will launch ..."

"With you on board?" Ziggy demanded.

Russ looked at her coldly. "Wouldn't you like to know?"

"Er, yes," said Ziggy, rolling her eyes, "that's why I asked."

- - - - -

"I shall tell you **nothing**!" Russ pressed another button on his remote. "I warned you that if I saw you again, I would show you no mercy."

The cages started to hum and whirr ...

And then they began to shrink!

"What's happening?" Ziggy spluttered as the contracting cage squashed her head between her knees.

"**These cages are going to crush us flat!**" A.D. gasped.

- - - - -

Escape to Danger

Adventure Duck braced himself against the steel bars of his shrinking cage. "We've been in some tight squeezes before, Ziggy ... but none quite as tight as *this*!"

"Tell me about it!" Ziggy's head was sticking out between her squashed-up legs. "What are we going to do?"

"I know!" came a voice from nowhere. **"CALL FOR CARRIE BOO!"** Suddenly the reindeer appeared beside the wicked walrus! Like a furry forklift truck she tucked her antlers under him and heaved with all her might, tipping the walrus over. The whole room shook as he fell, and the remote control clattered to the floor. Carrie kicked it over to Adventure Duck, who grabbed it with his wings.

"Good to see you, Carrie!" He pressed all of the buttons, and finally the cages switched off. With no magnetic pull holding the bars together, they fell to pieces.

"**FREEEEEEE!**" Neon Zebra leaped into the air and her stripes burned shocking pink. *ZAPPPP!* She blasted

Russ so hard that his tusks twitched and his moustache began to steam. "Care to join me, partner?"

"Don't mind if I do!" Adventure Duck spun the walrus round by his tusks and then let go. The walrus flew through the air – straight into the combined back hooves of Carrie and Ziggy! Lying on their backs, they pushed up together and propelled the

- - - - -

walrus – **SPLAT!** – into a wall.

"That does it." Russ flopped to the ground, his whiskers bristling with anger. "Now you've *REALLY* made me mad!"

"Uh-oh." Adventure Duck looked at his friends. "You know how this is a space base? Well, I think I'd like to put plenty of space between us and Russ! **RUN FOR IT!**"

"**You're all doomed!**" Russ roared, wobbling forward.

A.D. led Ziggy and Carrie in a mad charge back through the tunnel and out of the space base into the freezing cold.

"Hey, Carrie," said Ziggy. "That was a top rescue you pulled off!"

"I can't believe it worked," she said. "You guys are number ones when it comes to fighting crime – maybe Carrie Boo can be the number two!"

"I wouldn't want to *poo-poo* that plan," panted Adventure Duck. "Wait! Number two, you say? *That gives me a brilliant idea*." He flew up, circled over the hovercraft and unleashed a dozen deadly droppings! Soon, the craft was buried in the muck.

- - - - -

Ziggy held her nose. "UGH, GROSS!"

Carrie seemed impressed. "The meteor gave you *super-poo* too?"

"Nah, I was born this way." A.D. grinned. "Clever, eh? With Russ's hovercraft out of action, we can outrun him!"

"Where can we go?" wondered Ziggy. A snowstorm was blowing up, sending stinging flakes of snow into their faces. "We need to find shelter before we freeze to death."

"Let's head for the other building I spotted," said A.D. "Come on!"

The blizzard grew worse. Even with his insulated cape, A.D.'s beak chattered as he skied along on his webbed feet. Ziggy huddled close to Carrie as they ran, trying to get some extra warmth from the reindeer's shaggy fur.

At last the building came into sight through the howling storm. Ziggy skidded to a stop in front of it and frowned.

- - - - -

"**EWW!** Look at all that yellow snow! You know what that means."

A.D. turned up his beak. "The walrus did an enormous wee?"

"Look," said Carrie. "There's purple snow over here. And green snow just over there ..."

"I hear something coming," hissed Ziggy. "Everyone hide!"

Carrie disappeared while Adventure Duck and Ziggy lay down in the freezing snow. The next moment, a snowplough trundled out of the building, driven by an adorable little Arctic hare. It was fluffy and **pure white**, except for a GREEN STRIPE between its eyes ...

"Maybe I should get one of those stripes," A.D. murmured. "All the animals around here seem to have them."

The hare dug up the yellow snow with the plough's huge shovel. Then it carried off its frozen haul.

"Follow that little bunny," hissed Ziggy.

Stealthily, Adventure Duck, Neon Zebra and Carrie Boo trailed the snowplough as it drove into a big factory. They watched from behind some packing crates as the snowplough dumped the ice into a large vat. Yellow slush poured out into rows and rows of moulds – moulds in very familiar shapes ...

"*Rocket lollies,*" A.D. breathed.

Ziggy nodded. "That coloured snow is flavouring. Russ is using Arctic ice to make ice lollies."

"No, he isn't," came a prissy voice behind them. "**I am**. Delicious icy treats that will finally allow me to *take over the world*!

Adventure Duck and Neon Zebra – and possibly Carrie Boo (it was hard to tell since she'd turned invisible again) – spun round to find a small canine figure, bundled up in fleeces and furs.

It was Power Pug!

The Sinister
Snow-shifter

"**YOU!**" Ziggy scowled at Power Pug.

"I should have known you'd be around

here somewhere."

Power Pug preened.
"Because you
recognised the
GENIUS behind
my plan?"

"No, because it smells

like **DOG FARTS**!" Adventure Duck bunched his wings into fists. "I suppose Russ is working for you?"

"He is my *hench-walrus*," Power Pug confirmed smugly.

"I don't get it." Ziggy shook her head. "Why do you want to go to Mars? And why are you making all these ice lollies?"

"Unless they're to eat as in-flight snacks?" said A.D.

"You **SUPER-SIMPLETONS**!" Power Pug chuckled. "I will not use the spaceship to go to Mars. I will use it to orbit this world at super speed, bombarding the planet's population with my mind-control ice lollies ... or as I call them, **Mind-ControLLIES**."

"That is a *rubbish* name," Ziggy told him.

"To the humans, delicious icy treats falling from the sky will seem like a brilliant publicity stunt," Power Pug went on. "They will all eat my rocket lollies and fall into a trance."

"Like the crew of the space base," said Carrie Boo, turning visible again. "They just walked around in a daze. Nothing bothered them."

"Don't remind me." A.D. shuddered.

"My spaceship will cover the entire world in lollies!" Power Pug's voice was growing louder and more triumphant. **"I will take over the Earth and the humans will do my bidding without protest. I will be crowned KING PUG the ALL-POWERFUL!"**

"Um, what does Russ get out of all this?" A.D. wondered. "He seems super-smart – why would he want you in charge?"

Power Pug smiled craftily. "Perhaps he realises that *nothing* can stop me!"

"**EXCEPT US**," said Ziggy.

"We're *totally* going to stop you," Adventure Duck agreed.

"Is that so?" snarled Power Pug. "I reckon my meteorite-enhanced, utterly ruthless, evil-to-the-core hench-animal might have something to say about that."

"We already whopped your walrus," Carrie boasted.

"That big softie?" Power Pug snorted.

- - - - -

"I'm not talking about *him* ..." He clapped his paws and the bunny with the green stripe jumped down from the  snowplough, glaring at A.D. and the others. "I'm talking about **HIM**."

Adventure Duck snorted. "*THAT PIPSQUEAK?* What's he going to do, hit us with his *ickle paws*? Bop us with his *fluffy tail*?"

The hare's eyes flashed green. He blurred and then **morphed into a**

snarling white wolf,

with the same green stripe on his nose.

"**WHOA!**" A.D. jumped on to Ziggy, who jumped on to the invisible Carrie, who collapsed in a heap.

Power Pug chuckled. "You see, many meteorites fell here. One of them gave this magnificent beast the power to *change*

- - - - -

into ANY Arctic animal ... I call him the
SNOW-SHIFTER!"

"Wait a sec," A.D. breathed. "He was that bird I saw when I first arrived, wasn't he?"

"Now we know how those bird tracks turned into polar bear paw-prints," said Carrie, growing visible again. "They were made by the same creature!"

As if in agreement, the snow-shifter glowed again and grew even bigger – this time into a savage-looking **polar bear**! It let out an angry roar.

"My snow-shifter is the *perfect spy*!"

- - - - -

gloated Power Pug. "I knew you super-fools would try to spoil my plans so I sent him to keep a lookout ..." He pointed at Carrie Boo. "I didn't expect him to find me a THIRD hench-animal! Still, the more servants I possess the better." He looked at Carrie Boo with wide eyes that began to swirl and spiral. "**You are getting sleepy**," he whispered. "**When you wake you will OBEY me ... YOU WILL OBEY MEEEEEE ...**"

"**OH, NO, YOU DON'T!**" A.D. quickly gave a brain-cracking *QUACK!* in Carrie's ear – which broke the trance and turned her invisible. "You can't hypnotise what you can't see, *Pug-Ugly*!" He leaped on to Carrie's see-through back. "It's a lot harder to dodge her, too. **Yeeee-haaaa!**" Like a cowboy on a horse – or like a cow-*duck* on a *reindeer*, at any rate – A.D. rode Carrie right into the Snow-Shifter, knocking the bear backwards.

Neon Zebra fired a pulse of *pink neon energy* through her front hoof, knocking Power Pug's hat off and sending him staggering! Behind him, A.D. spotted an exit sign.

"**Let's roll!**" A.D. steered Carrie Boo through the factory doors, Ziggy galloping alongside them.

- - - - -

Outside, the snowstorm was still blowing.

"NOW what are we going to do?" asked
Carrie nervously.

"Something clever to stop Power Pug and
his super-thugs, of course!" said A.D. "*I'm
open to suggestions ...*"

Just then, the ground started to shake and
knocked them off their feet (and hooves).
A deep rumble, like a giant cracking its
knuckles, filled the air.

"Hey, what's going on?" cried Ziggy.

Carrie squealed. A dome of gleaming silver, as big as a football stadium, juddered up from under the ice right in front of them!

Ziggy's eyes were out on stalks. "**IT'S A FLYING SAUCER**!"

"It's the *top-secret spaceship*," A.D. realised. "It was parked out of sight all this time ... *until now.*"

Carrie gulped. "Because Russ the Walrus has made it ready to fly!"

Throbbing with energy, the flying saucer loomed above them – and *still* it went on rising. Twelve humungous rockets were stuck around the base – their sleek, red metal nose cones pointing up from titanic tubular bodies. Finally, the platform that supported the spaceship rose into sight, and with a **CLUNK** the rumbling stopped.

"No time to stop and stare," said Carrie, pointing behind them. "Big, hairy company – catching us up."

Roaring with rage, the polar bear snow-shifter charged across the ice with Power Pug on its back.

"There's nowhere to run, **SUPER-CREEPS**!" the pug ranted. "**YOU'RE GOING TO BE MY HENCH-ANIMAL'S DINNER!**"

With a bloodcurdling roar, the snow-shifter bared his super-sharp jaws, straining to devour them ...

A Whale of a Battle

Adventure Duck unwrapped his scarf and gave one end to Ziggy and the other end to Carrie. "Sorry, pug-face," he said. "I can't stand around here chatting with you all day. **GOTTA FLY!**"

He clamped his beak around the middle of the scarf. Flapping his wings with all his might, Adventure Duck took to the air through the driving snow, carrying his friends beneath him.

But Power Pug wasn't about to let them get away! The demented dog hopped off his hench-animal's back and screamed, "**Do something!**"

The polar bear glowed and blurred ... and suddenly turned into a gull with a familiar green stripe shining over his beak.

The gull flew with incredible speed, hovered over their heads – then turned back into a polar bear. "**ROARRRRRRRRR!**" The massive beast *plummeted down* and landed on top of Adventure Duck. All four animals struck the ice with a mighty **WHUMP**!

Ziggy blasted the polar bear backwards with

- - - - -

a neon-pink energy zap, putting some distance between them. But they'd hit the ground so hard, a jagged split appeared in the ice.

"Uh-oh," said A.D., watching as the crack grew bigger and bigger. Finally, the ice gave way and all the animals plunged down into freezing cold water!

SPLASH!

Despite the terrible temperature, A.D. was in his element now. As Ziggy and Carrie thrashed about, A.D. dived down and powered through the icy water.

He swam up to the polar bear, taking him
by surprise.

He used both webbed feet to super-kick the
beast in its butt, and the snow-shifter shot
through the water like a white torpedo.

Quickly, Adventure Duck swam back to the
surface and helped Ziggy and Carrie climb
on to a big floating iceberg.

"Thanks," said Ziggy through chattering
teeth. She fired up her stripes to warm
herself, but they sputtered and smoked. "Bad
news. **Neon power and water don't mix!**"

Carrie nodded her shaggy head. "And here comes that **wicked walrus** again!"

A.D. groaned. Russ the walrus was flopping over the ice towards them, sharp tusks glinting.

"This isn't good," said Carrie. "Walruses can swim really well."

"Don't worry. I'll get you out of here," Adventure Duck told his friends, summoning his super-strength to push them to safety.

But he never got the chance!

A colossal white whale broke

through the surface, spraying freezing-cold water from its blowhole. The bright green stripe on its nose was lost from view as the whale opened its mighty jaws wide to devour A.D. and his four-legged friends. It was the **SNOW-SHIFTER!**

Adventure Duck flapped away at the last moment. The whale jerked its head up out of the water, snapping at Adventure

- - - - -

Duck's tail feathers – and while it was distracted, Carrie and Ziggy lashed out with their forelegs. Their hooves caught the snow-shifter so hard that he flipped over backwards with an almighty **SPLASH!**

A.D. swooped down and grabbed the snow-shifter's whale-tail, hoping to spin it around. **WHUMP!** The whale batted Adventure Duck away, then dived back down into the water.

A.D. crash-landed on the glacier, bruising his butt on the hard ice.

"**LOOK OUT!**" cried Ziggy, pointing her hoof in warning.

- - - - -

The whopping walrus was slithering across the ice menacingly – right towards Adventure Duck!

"This is impossible!" Adventure Duck moaned. "I can't fight *both* of these whoppers at once!"

Suddenly Yoki's voice echoed through Adventure Duck's mind. "The walrus might *help* you, young duck."

"Help me? **As if!**" A.D. gasped.

The Wicked Walrus lunged for him, trying to spear him with his tusks. A.D. rolled clear and the walrus's tusks pierced the ice where he'd been a moment before, nearly turning him into a duck skewer. "If that's your best advice, Yoki, I wish you'd just clam up."

"It is the Snow-Shifter who must **clam** up," said Yoki. "If you understand my ingenious wordplay ...?"

A.D. dodged a flipper-strike from the deadly walrus – and suddenly smiled. "I think maybe I do, egg. Good pun!"

"I know!" Yoki said smugly. "I could be a stand-up comedian ..."

"Except you can't *actually* stand up,"

Adventure Duck pointed out.

"Legs are an illusion," Yoki said in a slight huff. "Now, young duck – it's time to put the **clam-plan** into action!"

In the water, the snow-shifter was still causing trouble. The white whale swam underneath Ziggy and Carrie's iceberg and tipped it over, sending them into the freezing water where they splashed helplessly.

"HEY! BLUBBER BRAINS!" A.D. yelled, perching on the overturned iceberg. "IS THAT A GREEN BOGEY ON YOUR NOSE?"

The whale rose menacingly from the water right in front of him, its eyes full of murder and fixed on Adventure Duck. But A.D. stared right back at the Snow-Shifter and continued to taunt him. "It's easy to turn into something really big. Any **zero** can do that!"

The whale slapped its tail against the water, creating a massive wave that swept Ziggy and Carrie up in its curl and deposited them on to the ice.

"What takes *REAL* skill is to turn into something teeny-weeny." A.D. challenged the whale, crossing his wings over his chest. "I bet you're **TOO STUPID** to do that, you **BIG BUFFOON**."

"A.D.'s lost it!" groaned Carrie.

"Don't provoke that thing," called Ziggy.

The Snow-Shifter laughed, then glowed and blurred. Its enormous whale's body twisted and shrank until all that was floating there was a **tiny clam** **with a green stripe on its shell.**

"That's pretty cool – for ME, not you." A.D. grabbed the clam and called out to the walrus. "Hey, Russ – what's a walrus's favourite food?"

- - - - -

"CLAMS!" cried Russ, his mouth opening automatically.

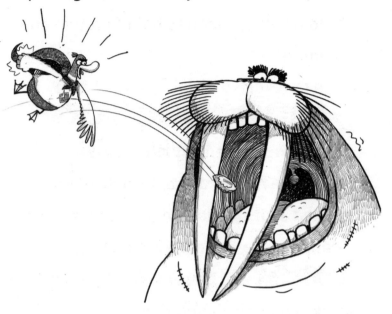

A.D. chucked the clam straight at the walrus. Russ caught it in his jaws, bit down with a **CRUNCH** and swallowed the snow-shifter down in one big, hungry gulp. Ziggy and Carrie cheered.

- - - - -

"The bad news is, you've eaten your fellow bad-guy," Adventure Duck told Russ. "The good news is, I bet he's full of protein and vitamins!"

"**NOOOOOOOOOO!**" Russ turned green. "**WHAT HAVE I DONE?**" The walrus's belly bulged and rippled as if a ball were bouncing around inside it. "Stop trying to change shape. *ARRRRRGH* ..." The walrus fell on his back, moaning and gurgling.

Adventure Duck smiled. "I guess something he ate disagreed with him!"

"There is no time to celebrate this victory,"

- - - - -

Yoki warned A.D. "I have been monitoring the situation. Power Pug is loading ice lollies into the giant spaceship."

"Cancel the celebrations, guys," A.D. groaned. "That prissy pug will be ready to take off any minute and put his plans into action!"

"Then he'll rule the world,"

wailed Carrie.

"Not on OUR watch!" Ziggy said.

"Too right," A.D. agreed. "We have to stop that pug – *before it's too late!*"

Rockets of Doom

As Adventure Duck, Ziggy and Carrie raced back to the launch pad, they saw Power Pug steering a hover-truck with his paws. He was dropping crate after crate of mind-control ice lollies into his stolen spaceship.

"We've taken care of your hench-animals ..." Adventure Duck shouted, flying at super-speed towards him. "*Now it's your turn, bum face.*"

"I hardly think so, you foul-mouthed water fowl!" Power Pug waited until A.D. had drawn close, then drove the hover-truck right into him. "**Take that!**"

One of the ice lolly crates broke over Adventure Duck's head. "**OOF!**" he quacked as he crashed into the snow in a hail of rainbow-coloured ice. He picked a bit of the wooden crate out of his beak. "That tastes a whole lot better than your dumb lollies."

Power Pug sneered. "Soon, all you will be tasting is *defeat*!"

"I'm going nowhere *near* your stinky feet,"

A.D. retorted, chuckling at his own joke.

"*The whole world will be at my feet!*"
Power Pug promised. "**My Mind-
ControLLIES will give me
mastery over all!**"

Another snowstorm was blowing up,
whipping freezing flakes in their faces.
Carrie helped A.D. stand up while Ziggy
glared at the hovering pug. "Without your
mates to help you, how will you steer your
ship and release your lollies, eh?"

Power Pug produced a remote. "The craft is
programmed to fly all around the world on
autopilot, dropping my lollies as I go."

- - - - -

"The only place you're going is **down**!"
Ziggy fired a smoking crackle of pink
energy from her hoof, but Power Pug
dodged the blast and pressed a button on
the remote.

"You're too late. I'm beginning take-off!"
crowed the pug.

"**NO!**" Carrie screamed.

The rockets rumbled, billowing smoke into the blizzard of snow, making it even harder to see anything. Power Pug jumped from his hover-truck on to the spaceship, and the abandoned vehicle dropped to the ground, almost squashing Adventure Duck.

"*At last, my dreams will come true!*" The diabolical dog clapped his little paws together. "The people of Earth will be my workforce, building incredible weapons and fleets of spaceships to my design. The world will become an *enormous* factory ... then I shall lead my human army into space and **CONQUER**

- - - - -

THE UNIVERSE! MWAH-HA-HAAAAAA!"

A.D. looked helplessly at Ziggy.

Ziggy looked helplessly at Carrie.

Carrie turned invisible; she could've been looking helplessly at anybody.

Then a huge figure slithered up through the smoke and snow.

"Hang on a minute, Power Pug." It was the walrus. He was still holding his belly, only now he didn't just have indigestion – he looked furious!

"**You said** your lollies would leave the humans unable to work. **You said** that they would shut all their factories and stop polluting the planet. **You said** that the environment would recover and that animals would rule it kindly."

"All *lies*, you blubbery buffoon!" Power Pug yelled down. "Thanks for your help. Take-off's in ten minutes." He entered the flying saucer through a hatch in the top and slammed it shut behind him. "Bye-bye, suckers!"

- - - - -

"**Oh, NOOO!**" Russ held his face in his flippers. "**What have I done?**"

"You've allowed that stupid mutt to take over the world!" said Ziggy.

"**He has not won yet**," Yoki's voice boomed through A.D.'s mind. "Power Pug can control the spaceship remotely, but it can also be controlled from—"

"*THE SPACE BASE!*" Adventure Duck blurted out loud. "Russ, we all want to stop Power Pug. How about we call a truce?"

Russ nodded. "Very well."

- - - - -

"Wait." Carrie looked at the walrus suspiciously. "How'd you get better so fast, anyway?"

"I passed the snow-shifter in my poop." Russ looked embarrassed. "The meteorite's powers keep me very regular—"

"PRIORITIES, PEOPLE!" Ziggy wailed.

A.D. nodded. "Russ, can we shut down Power Pug's launch from the space base?"

"Perhaps," said Russ. "If I can get there in time."

Ziggy jumped on to the abandoned hover-

- - - - -

truck. *"What are we waiting for?"*

"Go with Russ," said A.D. "That thing will move faster with just the two of you on board. Carrie and I will stay here and try to force our way inside that spaceship!"

"**We will?**" Carrie turned instantly invisible.

Ziggy and Russ piled on to the hover-truck. With a whir of motors it wobbled, rose up and sped away through the air.

"I have an idea," said A.D. Searching the broken-open crate of lollies, he found one that was lime flavour – and rubbed

- - - - -

the green ice on to his wing. "Power Pug doesn't know we've got rid of his Snow-Shifter, so I'm going to disguise myself with a **green stripe**."

Carrie considered A.D.'s plan. "He can only copy white animals though ..." She kicked snow all over A.D. "There you go!"

Adventure Duck blinked through the freezing white blanket of snow. "I look like a 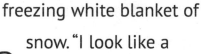 **SNOW-DUCK** - perfect!" He carried Carrie to the top of the

flying saucer and knocked on the door. "*Quick*, turn invisible so he doesn't suspect anything," whispered A.D. "You stop the take-off and I'll pound the pug."

"**Aha**," came Power Pug's voice from inside the spaceship as he peered through a peephole. "There you are, my snow-shifter. What kind of creature are you now? Not a very attractive one. No matter, you are just in time to join me on my maiden voyage ..."

Seeing no danger, Power Pug flipped open the hatch and stuck his head out.

POW*!* Adventure Duck attacked!

- - - - -

With a squeal of surprise Power Pug tumbled down into the flying saucer. Adventure Duck and Carrie jumped down after him.

THE FINAL BATTLE HAD BEGUN!

Take-Off and Take-Down

"Have some ice lollies!" cried
Power Pug, chucking a crate of them at
Adventure Duck.

"ONLY IF YOU TASTE MY FEATHERS,"
said Adventure Duck, swinging his wing at
Power Pug's flat-nosed face.

For once the pug wasn't hiding behind a
hench-animal. As Adventure Duck and his
nemesis traded kicks and punches among

the crates of ice lollies, the noise of the rockets outside built to a crescendo.

Carrie had turned visible again. She flicked the controls with her hooves. "**Help!**" she cried. "**I don't know what I'm doing!**"

Adventure Duck dodged a paw-punch

- - - - -

to the beak. "**FIND THE OFF SWITCH!**"

"There *is* no off switch," hissed Power Pug, ducking a wing-chop. "This is a highly advanced spacecraft controlled by a ***super-smart computer***."

"**SMASH THE COMPUTER!**" cried Adventure Duck.

"You'll never be able to destroy it in time," Power Pug gloated. With a bark of triumph, he booted Adventure Duck across the spaceship.

WHAM! A.D.'s butt landed on a bank of switches and they exploded in sparks.

At once, the rockets warbled worryingly. "Ouch," the duck groaned, rubbing his tail feathers. "What did I hit?"

Carrie peered at the switches. "The label says, *ROCKET ROTATORS.*"

"**NOOOOO!**" Power Pug scampered over a pile of crates and leaped on to the control panel. "Fix those switches. **Fix them now!**"

Across the glacier, Ziggy had steered the hover-truck through the snow to the **TOP SECRET SPACE BASE**.

Wasting no time, they went through the tunnel and into the mission control room. A big screen showed them the scene they'd left behind: the enormous spaceship juddering on its launch pad, surrounded by smoking rockets.

"STOP THOSE ROCKETS!" Ziggy yelled.

The walrus was already bashing at the switches and levers with his flippers. "I CAN'T!" he shouted. "Power Pug has locked down the systems! I can't get past the firewall without his password ... and I don't know what it is!"

- - - - -

Ziggy and Russ desperately typed possible passwords into the computer.

"Try, **POWERPUGROOLZ**!" Ziggy cried. "Try, **IHEARTPUGS**! Try, **PUGSROX1234**!"

"Wrong, *wrong*, **wrong**," Russ blubbered.

Ziggy looked back at the big computer screen – and frowned. The rockets stuck to the sides of the spaceship were spinning round wildly.

Ziggy was baffled. "What's going on? How come they're turning all over the place like that?"

"The rockets can turn in any direction required to steer the spacecraft," said Russ. "Wait ... rotating rockets. That could be the answer!" Russ clapped his flippers and barked like a sea lion. "If the rockets launch while they're upside down, their jets will fire harmlessly into the air."

Ziggy felt excited. "They'll push Power Pug's spaceship *down* into the ice instead of up into the sky. That'll really sink his plans!"

"But only if I can hack inside the systems and position the rockets correctly." Russ typed **TOPPUG***! and got another error message. "Ohhhh," he groaned in frustration, "What *is* his password ... ?"

- - - - -

"Try, **PASSWORD**," suggested Ziggy.

"Seriously?" Russ typed it in – and gasped as he was rewarded with a loud bleep. "**It works**! I'm through the firewall. I can take control of the spaceship's systems!"

"**WAY TO GO!**" yelled Ziggy.

Back on board the spacecraft, Power Pug jumped up and down on the levers and switches. "I'm locked out of my own systems!" he wheezed. "It's impossible. **It's an outrage!**"

"It's the best news I've heard all day," Adventure Duck declared.

- - - - -

With a snarl, Power Pug snapped off a lever and lunged at A.D.

Carrie bravely stepped in front of him.

"Out of my way, deer," jeered Power Pug. "Why don't you do yourself a favour and disappear – before I *make* you disappear."

But instead of turning invisible, Carrie socked Power Pug with her hoof, slamming him to the floor. "YOU CAN'T SCARE ME, POOPY-FUR!" she shouted. "After today, I'm not scared of ANYTHING."

Adventure Duck beamed. "Then let's make sure there's a tomorrow!" Leaving the pug

- - - - -

where he lay unconscious, A.D. grabbed Carrie by the antlers, lifted her up through the hatch in the roof – and slammed it shut behind them. He could hardly see a thing for thick smoke. The roar of the rotating rockets was frighteningly loud.

"3 ... 2 ... 1 ... LIFT OFF!" Adventure Duck shouted, soaring into the air holding Carrie by her antlers.

They had almost reached the **TOP SECRET SPACE BASE** when the wrong-way-round rockets finally fired. For a few seconds, twelve huge plumes of flame lit up the Arctic sky like candles on a giant birthday cake. Then the flying saucer forced

- - - - - -

its way through the ice with a breathtaking

When the smoke had cleared and the
ground had stopped shaking, the spaceship
and even the launch pad itself had
disappeared.

"It's over," Carrie breathed, peering into the
gigantic hole in the ice.

Adventure Duck whooped. "**WE JUST SAVED THE ARCTIC!**"

"We really did!" yelled Ziggy, running over to join them with Russ. She did a strange wobbly victory dance. "**OH, YEAH! UH-HUH!**"

The reindeer joined in. "Carrie Boo says **Hip-Hip-HUROOOOOOOO!**"

"Thank goodness I took control of Power Pug's systems in time," said Russ.

"You did great, flipper face!" A.D. high-fived the walrus, and Russ held out his other flipper for a down-low.

- - - - -

"Well, what do you know." Ziggy grinned.
"They started as **FOES**, and now they're
BROS!"

Carrie turned to A.D. "Was Power Pug
definitely on the spaceship when it
went down?"

"I couldn't tell because of all the smoke. But
hopefully that's the last we'll see of him."
Adventure Duck grinned. "What about you,
Carrie – will we see you again?"

"Everyone will see me!" Carrie vowed.
"I know how to control my powers now,
so I'm going to go back to my herd and look
after them."

"Wait," said A.D. "What about the space base and the people who work here?"

"I shall let them move back in," said Russ. "When the **Mind-ControLLIES** wear off, none of them will remember what happened. They can return to their research."

"And you, Russ?" wondered Ziggy. "What will you do now?"

The walrus smiled. "I shall roam the Arctic quietly, using my powers to protect this beautiful place."

"Sounds good," said Adventure Duck. "As for

- - - - -

me, I think I'm going to kick back and relax. Maybe take a little holiday—"

"There is much work to do, young duck," said Yoki's voice in A.D.'s head. **"You and Ziggy must return home."**

"OH, C'MON!" A.D. pouted. "The world must be safe from bad guys for a while."

"Perhaps so," the egg agreed. "But the Underpond does not dust itself, you know!"

A.D. sighed. "All right, Ziggy – I *suppose* we'd better be going."

- - - - -

They said goodbye to Russ and Carrie, then Adventure Duck flapped into the sky – towing Ziggy along with his scarf.

"I'm looking forward to getting back to the warm," said Ziggy.

"Me too." Adventure Duck smiled. "My nose is froze ... my knees be freeze ... and I really can't tell you what's gone numb ..."

THE END

STEVE COLE

Bestselling author Steve Cole comes from a village with three different duck ponds. None of them has been hit by a meteor, but a duck did attack him once! When he's not writing funny stories, Steve performs with the pop band Faces Fall. Steve has a pet dog named Clara, who luckily does not possess evil mind-control powers. The superpower Steve would most like is the ability to conjure chocolate and chips from thin air (not always at the same time).

ALEKSEI BITSKOFF

Illustrator Aleksei Bitskoff was born in Estonia and loved to draw as a child, covering his school exercise books in doodles. He planned to become a teacher, but his travels brought him to London where he studied illustration instead. The superpower he would like most is self-multiplication, so he could be in lots of different places at the same time!

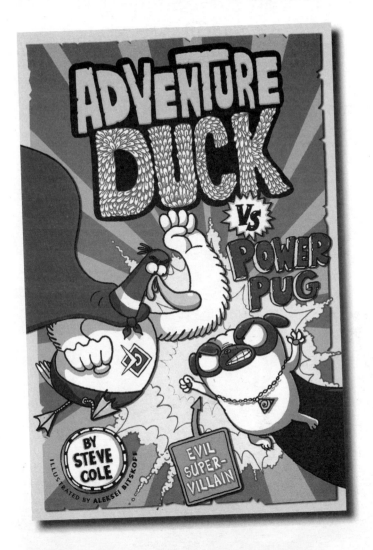

HAVE YOU READ ADVENTURE
DUCK'S FIRST BOOK?

IT'S GUARANTEED TO
QUACK YOU UP!

THE BATTLE IS ON . . .

DUCK FOR COVER!